THE URBAN STORY CAUGHT UP

BOOK 1

Sylvester Murray

Copyright © 2020

By Sylvester Murray

All rights reserved. This book or any portion thereof may not be reproduced or used in any manner whatsoever without the express written permission of the publisher except for the use of brief quotations in a book review.

TABLE OF CONTENT

CHAPTER ONE 2

CHAPTER TWO 16

CHAPTER THREE 33

CHAPTER FOUR 51

CHAPTER FIVE 67

CHAPTER ONE

The night was dark and windy. But Deshawn felt a body close by that made him not feel so cold. He was tethering on that brink of sleep and wakefulness. For a second, he didn't know who was beside him or where he was. Even in his subconscious state, he observed that he was not in his bed. It scared him and he woke up with a start. He reached beside him for his Glock 22 – he always kept it handy whenever he was asleep. The gun made him feel safe, and without it by his side, he couldn't go to sleep. He clutched it to his chest as he gradually realized where he was. He was at B'onca's apartment. He didn't like sleeping there, but that night he had somehow felt compelled to B'onca asked him.

B'onca had somehow managed to infiltrate his life. In terms of relationships with women, he always avoided getting attached. He could have a casual fling with them, but never something serious. He still found it strange that he had gotten serious with a woman. He often wondered what attracted him to B'onca. He knew that it wasn't her looks, even though she was drop-dead gorgeous. She was 5'3" with full lashes that looked seductive when she blinked. Her brown skin was smooth and soft. She had an oval face, slanted eyes, and a nose that rounded off perfectly at the tip. She had honey colored eyes. Her lips were full and luscious, Deshawn always teased her by saying that they begged to be kissed. She had beautiful long, black hair that reached her shoulders, which she braided most of the time.

But, it wasn't just her looks that pulled him to her. There was something else, something that he could not explain. There was something about her, the way she talked, walked, and even touched things had the most unusual effects on him. He loved her confidence, the way she always cared about the next person, and the way she always set out to accomplish whatever she put her mind to. The last part was something that they both had in common, he was no less determined than she was.

He could never forget the first day they met at a friend's party. She had looked so amazing that night and he couldn't stop himself from going over to talk to her. And ever since that night, he had become hooked to her. More hooked than he could dare admit.

He hated himself for caring so much about B'onca and their child in the next room. He wondered what had happened to the old him, and when he suddenly grew so soft. Maybe it was fatherhood that had softened him, or perhaps this part of him had been lurking beneath the tough appearances that he often put up. Maybe this was the real him, the tough-guy side that he usually showed people might be to mask how soft he was, and to keep himself from getting trampled underfoot. He turned to his side to have a better view of the woman that was next to him. Her dark hair was spread out in a disorganized fashion across her back. With the dim light in the room, he could see the outline of her body.

Her nightdress wasn't so loose fitting so it traced the curves of her body as it went. Her hair smelt of strawberries.

From where he lay, he could see her side heaving up and down as she slept. Her back was to him so he could not see her face but he knew that she looked beautiful. She always looked beautiful while she slept. Like a goddess that was oblivious of everything else that went on in the world. He often stared at her while she slept when he happened to wake in the middle of the night like this and she was facing him.

Earlier that night, when she had begged him to stay for dinner, she had informed him that their daughter, Britney, would soon be turning four. He was surprised when she said it, but he did not want to show it. What kind of father didn't know that his child was about to turn four? He found it difficult to believe that he had been a father for four years. Time flew so fast and it seemed like only yesterday when B'onca had told him that she was pregnant, and now look at him, he was the father of a soon to be four-year-old.

His daughter was a spitting image of her mother. She had her dark hair and honey colored eyes, with the same smooth and silky brown skin. The girl did not seem to have any of his qualities physically, but according to the stories that B'onca told him, she acted like him. B'onca had often told him about how stubborn she was and how difficult it was raising her alone. B'onca virtually raised their daughter by herself, though not in terms in finance. He contributed more than his fair share when it came to the money, but he knew what she was talking about. He was never there as a father figure for his daughter.

As a matter of fact, the little girl could count how many times she had seen him. Though he had actually come to see her more times than she knew, he often came late at night when the little girl and sometimes even her mother had gone to sleep. When he came in at such late hours, he would go up to his daughter's room to see her, before dropping a wad of cash in an envelope on the kitchen counter.

More baffling was the fact that he had also been with the same woman for six years. He never believed that he could stick around that long in a relationship. Before he met B'onca, the maximum that his relationships lasted was a year, which he considered to be a long relationship. He was the type who loved having short term flings with women and then moving on, no strings attached. But with B'onca it was different. Something about her had attracted him, and did not just attract him, but managed to tie him down. Sometimes he racked his brain to pinpoint exactly what it was that tied him to her in such a way, but he was unable to arrive at anything.

B'onca turned around to face him in her sleep. She peered at him from her dreamland with eyes that were barely open. Then her eyes opened wider as she saw the gun that he clutched to his chest. "Shawn, what is that gun doing on this bed? You know the rules."

Deshawn opened a drawer on the nightstand next to the bed, and put the gun in there. He had spent hours in B'onca's apartment, and it worried him. He had many enemies, and he didn't want them to know about B'onca and his child. They could easily use his family against him just as he'd done to countless others. In his line of work, you do not give the enemies something to use against you. He had to leave her apartment. He had spent too much time there already. But, he would wait until B'onca was sound asleep again, then he would leave.

Waiting was painful. He heard every tick of the clock in the bedroom as he waited for B'onca to sleep. After some time, when he believed that an hour must have passed, he got up quietly from the bed. He tip-toed out of the room and shut the door behind him gently. He went to his daughter's room to have a look at her before he left. If he did not see her then, he might not get the opportunity to see her again soon. She was sound asleep when he came in. The room was dark save for the red night light in the room which cast a red glow over everything. Britney was hugging Bernard, her favorite teddy bear, to her chest while she slept. Bernard was the teddy bear that he had gotten her when she had turned two. She had been so excited when he bought her the teddy, and he was quite pleased with himself. At least he was able to get her something that she loved.

After standing for a while watching her sleep, he moved to her bedside and kissed her cheek, then he left the room as quietly as he could. He stepped gently on the wooden stairs to prevent them from creaking. Once downstairs, he unlocked the door that led out of the apartment with his own key and then locked it as soon as he was out of the apartment. He started walking briskly away from the apartment, and whipped out his phone from his pocket to call Carlos. The night was cold and it hit him hard as he walked.

He told Carlos to pick him up a few blocks from where he was. He increased his pace in an effort to get rid of the dreadful cold that was settling into his bones. He just wished that Carlos would be at the rendezvous when he got there, and he would not have to stand and wait for him long. But Carlos was a trustworthy lad, he assured himself. Carlos kept to time like a clock.

About three minutes after Deshawn got to where he was supposed to meet Carlos, a black BMW pulled up next to him. The glasses were tinted so you could not see anyone inside the vehicle, no matter how much you looked. He opened the back door and got in. Carlos was behind the wheel. The warm leather seat comforted him in contrast to the bitter cold outside the car. The car heater was turned on, and he knew that in a couple of minutes he would be feeling warm again.

"Good evening, boss, "Carlos greeted. "Where to?"

"Take me home, Carlos," he replied.

Carlos was one of his boys that he had taken a special fancy to. He loved the way that Carlos always kept to time and was always available to come pick him up at any hour he called. Though considering the relationship between him and Carlos, Carlos didn't really have much of an option than to come running when he called. But, he liked the way Carlos did it, always smiling and never complained about the inconveniences that came with the job.

Carlos was a young South American he had recruited into the team along with his twin brother, Tobias. They were both from Brazil and had come to the United States years ago with their parents in search of a better life. Things didn't go as planned, however. Their mother died soon after they arrived, and their father who never recovered from the impact of her death took to drinking. He drank so much he would sometimes fall sleep on the road while returning home. When he managed to successfully return to the one room apartment they lived in, he would sleep outside the door because he couldn't open the door in his drunken state. Carlos and his brother awoke many mornings to find him outside the door, snoring noisily.

Their father had made them feel ashamed. The neighbors would often pass him while he lay outside the door, stinking of alcohol and muttering in his sleep. He later died of liver disease. It wasn't long before Carlos and Tobias took to a life of crime. They broke into people's apartments and shops and stole stuff. They were only fifteen years old then. They had been in and out of several juvenile homes before Deshawn found them. He took them under his care and gave them jobs. He was, however, founder of Carlos. They were twenty at the time.

Deshawn, too, had a rough childhood, so he understood their plight. Though he didn't have a drunkard of a father who slept on the staircase, he was constrained as a child. He never got to hang out with other kids and do what they did. He was always confined indoors with his brother. His brother had somehow adapted to their upbringing and became the "perfect son" His brother obeyed all the rules set by their strict parents and even snitched on Deshawn when he broke them. His parents were disciplinarians to the core and there was never an acceptable excuse for breaking a laid down rule.

He, however, wanted to be free. The rules were choking the life out of him. What made him angry the most was that whenever he misbehaved or did something that his parents did not approve of, they would always refer to how well behaved his younger brother, Michael, was. Though his parents provided him with everything that he needed, nothing he did ever seemed to please them. He had been labelled the black sheep of the family. All in all, there was never much love in their home. When he got older, he left home and moved in with his uncle, against his father's wishes. But at that point, he cared less what his father thought. His uncle was a well-known drug lord who took him in and showed him the ropes of the business. He was a fast learner, and when his uncle felt that he could handle it, he put him in charge of distribution in a area.

Many of the people who had been working for his uncle were not so pleased about that. Many of them had been with his uncle for years and were yet to be promoted to such a position. The jealousy was natural, but he didn't let any of it get to him. Anyone who attempted to undermine his authority or sabotage him was quickly crushed. He felt it was necessary to send a message across to them – he would not tolerate nonsense. Swift and brutal consequences awaited anyone who tried to cross him.

As Carlos drove on, his building came into view. It was located on a hilltop that gave him an amazing view of the city of Detroit. The house looked beautiful, especially at night when all the outside lights were turned on. The lights glowed from a distance like beacons in the night. The house was big and beautiful, but it didn't feel like home to him. Home was where people that you loved were. In that place, there was no one that he really loved. Just him and his boys. He remembered the one-story that he had previously lived in. It was a house in a neighborhood that bubbled with life and families. That kind of neighborhood was also the perfect cover for his illegal business. But then, the house got raided and destroyed. In his short life, he had seen a lot of people die.

When he started managing a part of his uncle's business, he moved out of his uncle's mini mansion and into an apartment. Things were moving quite well. He had a right-hand man, Scott. He was the one who coordinated a lot of things about the business. He mainly supervised him and made sure that everything was in order. They had run the business for over a year before trouble came calling. The police acting on some anonymous tip, had decided to raid the house. Scott and another guy who was in charge of delivery in the nearby neighborhood had been in the living room talking about business. On the table in front of them was cocaine, wrapped up neatly and ready for distribution. Deshawn had excused himself to get something outside and when he was returning the front door burst open.

A team of heavily armed policemen stormed into the flat, flashing torches around. They ordered everybody to get down on the ground. Deshawn sighted them early enough and was lucky to have escaped. He later learned that Scott had made to reach for his gun and was shot by the police. He later died in the hospital. The other guy was taken into custody and sentenced. Deshawn had gone underground for a while after that so things could cool off. He was, however, forced to return sooner than he had planned when his uncle died, and he had to take over the business. He became more successful than his uncle, and expanded the cartel even more. He did not have to live in an apartment anymore, he bought himself a mansion and lived like the drug lord he was.

The car pulled up in front of his gate. Several of his security guards were on duty. Carlos rolled down the glass and placed his finger on a screen held out by one of the guards. Afterwards, the gate opened and the car drove into the compound. The driveway from the gate to his house was long, nearly five hundred meters. Carlos often said that an Olympics Marathon could be organized on the driveway.

The mansion consisted of eight en-suite bedrooms. Three on the ground floor, and five on the first floor. It had two living rooms, one store, one laundry room, a library, and a study. The floor of the entire building was covered with marble. The ceilings were high, and chandeliers dropped from them. The living room downstairs had three French windows. Two were located on the East side of the room, while one was located on the South. The furniture in the house was stylish and there were life size art paintings on the walls. Deshawn sometimes felt that there was too much empty space in the house. There were bedrooms that he had not entered for weeks.

As the car drove up to the house, Deshawn observed that everywhere was dark and it looked like no one was up. Not that he was expecting anyone to be up that early in the morning. The car stopped in front of the house, and he got out before Carlos drove to the garage to park the car. As soon as he stepped out of the car, the light of the lobby came on. The door swung open, and his butler was standing with a smile on his face to welcome him home, surprising Deshawn.

The butler, Marcus, was an Irishman that had moved to the United States from Ireland. He was in his late fifties and had white, wooly hair. He was over six feet tall, but a slight stoop in his posture reduced his height. He served in the British Army for a long time, before being honorably discharged when he developed a health condition that made it impossible for him to remain in the army. He had then moved to the US, where he worked for a while as a security guard and subsequently a housekeeper before Deshawn employed him to be his butler. He had a nose that curved sharply at the tip, reminding one of the beak of a bird. His smile however made up for that – he had a nice dentition, which he revealed when he smiled. Though he did not know it, his smile was one of the reasons Deshawn hired him. Nothing like a beautiful smile to welcome a guest.

Marcus had Deshawn's favorite cocktail and a cigar on a tray. Just what he needed at the moment, Deshawn thought to himself. He never got tired of drinking gin with lemon juice, orange bitters and simple syrup. He took the glass from the tray and downed it in one long gulp. He patted Marcus's back as he lit the cigar, and puffed at it as he went upstairs to his room to change. He felt tired, and some of the cold that had clung to him when he had left B'onca's apartment to wait for Carlos had not left yet. He removed all his clothes, and though it was three in the morning, he decided to have a bath before diving into his bed.

When he came out from the bathroom, he felt better. He no longer felt cold. He sat on his bed smoking, while his brain wandered out to think of certain things. Things like the birthday of his daughter, which the nature of his work might not even permit him to go and see her. He wanted to see her on her birthday, it was her special day. She had grown so fast. If someone had told him six years ago that he would be a father of a four-year-old girl in less than seven years, he would never have believed it. He had the money, and sticking to one woman for so long had never been his thing.

He liked to have a good time, and then leave. He didn't want either him or the girl to start attaching any feelings to the relationship. It was simply one of mutual benefit. With his success and wealth, he found it hard to differentiate between girls that loved him for him, and the ones that were after his money. It was difficult to decide, since all of them were always there for him, always willing to do things for him. Some of them did it, because they loved him and valued him. The others did it because they knew that he was rich, and they wanted to be in good standing with him so that they could cash in on it if the opportunity ever came. He understood this only too well, and they were part of his reasons for not wanting a relationship.

But, all that changed when B'onca came into the picture. With her, he didn't want to leave. He was even scared of her leaving him, though he'd rather get shot in the leg than admit it in her presence. That was something else that bothered him. He was starting to care too much, and visit her and his daughter too often. He was running the risk of them being discovered, and probably by someone who would want to use it against him.

He even kept their existence away from members of his cartel. He did not let them know where his family lived, for fear that one day they might betray him. In his world, sometimes loyalty changed when money was involved. He knew people that would be willing to pay a large sum for information like that. And if people in his cartel knew where his family was, some of them might be tempted to talk for the right price. Even Carlos, whom he was very close to, didn't know. He would always have Carlos drop him a distance from the house while he walked the rest of the distance to the apartment, keeping to the shadows. When he wanted to leave the apartment, he would also walk a couple of blocks before calling Carlos to come and pick him up.

The relationship between him and his daughter also bothered him. Having grown up in a family that didn't really care for him in any other way apart from financially, he didn't want to be the kind of father that his own father was.

His father had been terrible at fatherhood, and when he was a kid he had promised himself that whenever he became a father, he would do better. Here he was, it seemed he was doing even worse. He loved Britney no doubt, but the nature of his business was one that required him to be away from her most of the time. He did send her gifts when he could though, and he hoped those gifts would tell her how much he loved her.

His king size bed called to him. He glanced at the clock on the nightstand, an hour had passed by. He didn't know that he had been sitting up for that long. That next day was going to be a busy day at work, and he needed to get some sleep if he was to function optimally. He had about two hours and some minutes to sleep before he left the house for the office. Luckily for him, he had slept quite a bit at B'onca's place.

He lay down on the silky sheets and covered himself up with the blanket. He smelt the sweet fragrance of his pillows as he laid his head on one. It was not long after his head touched the pillows that he slept off.

He had a dream. In the dream, he was with his daughter in a field, somewhere sunny. She was wearing a red dress while he was dressed in a pair of denim jeans and a white shirt. She had a hat on her head, and he had snatched her hat and ran off. She trotted after him, he knew that she was never going to catch up, so after a while, he turned around and swept her into his arms. They were both laughing and sweating. As he carried her in his arms, she reached for her hat, took it off his head, and placed it on her own head

CHAPTER TWO

Deshawn woke up feeling groggy. He wasn't sure if he was still dreaming or was awake for a while. The dream had seemed so real, and for a while he wished that it was real. The joy that he had felt with being with his daughter was something that he missed badly. He rarely spent time with his daughter, and after the dream, the feeling that he was neglecting her became more acute. The fact that he had also not slept much the previous night, made it difficult for him to leave his bed. It was like his bed had developed arms, and held him down. He felt like going back to sleep, but he knew that there was work to do. Work that couldn't wait. The success of his business empire depended on his scheduled regularity to the office.

He pressed the intercom button and asked for his breakfast to be brought up. After a few minutes, Marcus came into the room carrying his breakfast on a tray. He set it down on a table next to the bed and greeted Deshawn with a smile. "How are you Marcus?" Deshawn asked.

"Very well sir," he replied.

Deshawn loved people who did their jobs cheerfully. The same reason that he had taken to Carlos was the same reason that he liked Marcus. Marcus was dedicated to his duties, and carried them out promptly. He would even go the extra mile of anticipating his needs and making provisions for them. Just like the previous day when he had returned in the early hours of the morning, he was not expecting Marcus to meet him at the door. He had even concluded that Marcus was asleep, and that he would not wake him up. He would leave him to sleep, but Marcus had been there with a lit cigar and his favourite cocktail, to welcome him. He had hired Marcus three years ago, and since then, he hadn't had any reason to regret the decision.

Marcus left the room after dropping the food on the table. As Deshawn bit into the food, he couldn't help nodding his head in delight. The toast tasted so good that if he didn't have somewhere to be, he would have ordered that more be brought up. He finished the toast and the cup of coffee and cream that was brought up. He pressed the intercom again to tell Marcus that he was done eating and that he should bring up his clothes. After speaking into the intercom machine, he went into the bathroom to have a shower. He felt better after eating, and the feeling of grogginess that had besieged him all morning finally left him.

As the water ran over his skin, his mind drifted off to his office and the pile of work that was waiting for him. He had an incoming shipment of drugs from Africa, and they were a lot of things to put in place to make sure that everything went smoothly. Nothing could be left to chance, there could be no loose ends. When it came to business, he couldn't really trust anyone to handle things perfectly, except himself. He was a goal getter and usually accomplished whatever he set out to accomplish. He washed his body, and then turned off the shower.

When he stepped out of the bathroom, he observed that the items he used for his breakfast were no longer there.

There was a navy-blue three-piece suit on his bed, with a white shirt. He put on the pants first, before putting on the white shirt and tucking it in. Next, he put on the waistcoat, before he slipped into the jacket. He walked to where his shoes were and selected a black brogue. Then he stood in front of the full-length mirror in the bedroom, and looked at himself, he looked good as always. He thought maybe he would look better if he put on a tie, but he quickly thrust the idea from his mind. He looked great, and moreover he didn't have any time to waste. Not like putting on a tie would actually waste his time, but he knew that he would have a hard time selecting a tie from his array of ties, and he didn't want to put himself in that situation at the moment.

He stepped out of his room, and made his way down the arched staircase. When he opened the front door, Carlos was already waiting for him with the car. Gone was the BMW of the previous night, in its place was a black Mercedes E53 Sedan AMG. The windows were as tinted as those of the BMW, if not more tinted. Carlos opened the door for him, and greeted him as he stepped into the car. Carlos then got in and started the engine. Jamie, one of his guards, was in the front seat of the car. Carlos drove out of the gate and sped towards the direction of his office.

At the office, as expected, there was a lot of work to be done. There were calls to be made, dealers to be paid and a lot of other business-related matters. He made a call to one person, before replying to another's email, and then approving payment for another. There didn't seem to be an end to the work. He decided he would just do what was necessary and leave the rest for another day, or probably delegate someone else to do it. He worked until it was evening. He called Carlos to have him bring the car to the front of the building. The car was waiting for him when he got down, Jamie was seated in the front seat, just like in the morning.

As the car made its way to Deshawn's house, he thought about his childhood. A lot had changed since then. He never thought as a child that he would end up in his line of business. Though as a child, he wasn't even allowed to think. His parents had been the ones doing his thinking for him, up until the time he left them. They had always tried to bend his will into theirs. With them, he couldn't be himself. He always had to conform to the standards that were expected of him. That was something that he had gotten tired of. Living to please others.

Deshawn had come from a strict but wealthy family. His father owned a small chain of grocery stores. They had a store in three different states, and his father ran the three of them from the main store that was only a few blocks away from their house. His mother stayed at home with him and his brother. His parents put them in the most prestigious schools around, not minding the cost. They made sure that him and his brother signed up for every extracurricular activity possible. Him and his brother never seemed to have any time for themselves. Their parents often reminded them that they didn't spend money on them and their education just to have other kids come out on top in school. Though his parents spent a lot of money on him and his brother, there wasn't much love between any of them. The money was the only thing that his parents actually did provide, in terms of moral support and things like that, they were never available.

His mother was a strict woman who never tolerated any form of "nonsense." She wouldn't put up with any kind of messing around. She always saw to it that him and his brother spent their time in a "useful" way. Their parents had drawn up timetables for them at a very young age. Time tables which they were expected to follow rigidly. There could be no extenuating circumstance for not keeping to the time table, apart from being sick or injured. Him and his brother could read fluently by the time they got to five years of age. They could read and write both English and Spanish.

His father wasn't around often, he was usually busy managing his stores. But when he was home, he would grill his wife and children on what they had accomplished and learned while he was away. If Deshawn or his brother had misbehaved, they would get a beating from their father. To them, he had become the symbol of justice. As a child, his father had been the person that he had been most terrified of. Not only because of his rigid discipline, but also because his rules seemed to be set in stone. There was no room for excuses or amendments.

He remembered a day he had snuck out of the back door of their house while he was supposed to be reading in his room. He was seven years old then. He wanted to play with the neighborhood kids who were having a street hockey tournament. He had played with them for a while before his mother appeared on the scene. He was shocked when he saw her. He thought he had finally gotten an opportunity to enjoy what he was denied most times, the opportunity to play with other kids in the neighborhood. When his mother found him in roller blades two sizes too big for him, racing up and down their street with a stick, she lost it. All she had to do was to make eye contact with him and give him the warning look that stopped him dead in his tracks, he threw off the roller blades and ran into the house.

Forgiveness was an alien word in their home, and he paid the full price for his sin. He had to kneel down on uncooked rice that his mother spread on the hardwood floors of their house until his father got home. He knelt there in agony for more than an hour. When his father had come back, he had pleaded with him to show him mercy, but all that was written on his father's face was disappointment. There was no amount of crying, begging or agonized facial expression, that would make them change their minds about something, especially when it had to do with discipline. They believed that children, and in fact everyone, should be made to face the consequences of their actions. No cutting corners.

When he was twelve he followed some of his friends to the cinema to see a movie after school. He didn't inform his parents, not like they would have approved if he had told them. They hardly approved of anything that was not related to academics. To them, such an outing was a waste of time. The hours spent to see a movie, could have been spent memorizing a formula or solving equations. The movie ended up taking more time than Deshawn had thought it would, and he returned home about three hours late from school. His mother was sitting next to the door waiting for him. She had pulled him by the ear as soon as he stepped into the house. She dragged him to the living room and made him kneel there while she thought of an appropriate punishment. When she let go of his ear, it was throbbing with pain. For the next couple of minutes, his ear felt like it belonged to someone else.

He had asked his brother to cover for him. He told him to tell their parents that they had extra science lessons after school. His brother, however, had gotten home and told his mother that he didn't know where he had gone off to with his friends. His mother got even more infuriated when she found out that it was a cinema. She slapped his cheek twice. When his father came back and was told what he had done, he received a whipping from his father. While whipping him, his father called him a fool several times.

From that day on he stopped telling his brother anything or asking favors from him. They became more like strangers living in the same house. His brother somehow managed to conform to all the expectations of their parents, and always act according to their wishes. He couldn't, his kind of spirit that wanted to be free didn't allow him. Many times, his parents search lights were mainly on him. They didn't monitor his brother so much, because they believed that even without supervision he would do the right thing. He was the one who needed constant monitoring to ensure that he was doing the right thing.

After the cinema incident, the little freedom that he enjoyed was revoked. He was no longer allowed to go anywhere without the company of his brother. His parents believed that his brother would always give them the true report about everything. His brother became more or less their parent's CCTV camera that watched over him all the time. It was annoying, but there was little he could do about it. It was only when he graduated from high school that he was allowed some measure of freedom again.

Deshawn's father had a brother who visited occasionally. He was wealthier than his father. For reasons he did not understand at the time, his father never talked about his brother if he could help it. He always changed the topic whenever his brother was brought up. Whenever their uncle came to visit, he always showed special attention to Deshawn. Their uncle seemed to admire Deshawn's spirit of adventure. Deshawn was always willing to try out new things and explore, he hated to be confined to one place and be told what to do, unlike his brother. His brother had become more or less their parent's lap dog. Deshawn's brother couldn't do a thing without seeking the approval of their parents first, and everything he ever did reflected their parent's wishes.

Deshawn's uncle became his greatest role model. He drove the nicest cars which seemed to change on a regular basis and was always impeccably dressed in suits which Deshawn admired. His uncle would always get him toys and sneak them to him when his parents weren't looking and his tell-tale brother was out of sight. His uncle also taught him tricks on how to control surrounding people. Though none of the tricks actually worked then –he had tried to get rid of his parent's way of monitoring him, but had failed.

One day when Deshawn asked him what kind of work he did, his uncle had replied that he "controlled the people around him." Deshawn didn't understand exactly what his uncle meant, but he knew that he wanted the confidence and money his uncle had. He wanted to be rich and independent, and not continue to live in his parent's shadow. He wanted to be his own man and he secretly longed for when he would become like his uncle. He had to wait quite a long time, but eventually his dreams come true.

Like his father wanted him to, Deshawn studied a business course in school. His father had been the one paying for his fees and he couldn't go against his wish. When he graduated, he told his father that he had no intention of managing the family business or taking over. He told them that his uncle had a place for him in his line of work. His father had been infuriated and had threatened to do all sorts of things to Deshawn if he took up with his uncle. But by then, Deshawn no longer cared what his family thought about his decisions, especially his father.

True to his threat, his father cut him off from all finances of the family when he left. His father had even threatened to disown him if he did not come back. None of that bothered him, and his father soon realized that and let him be. He sometimes wondered why they even bothered with trying to make him take over the family business. He was the supposed black sheep of the family. They should have made their sweet perfect son take over instead. Deshawn became his uncle's apprentice; his uncle was one of the most powerful drug lords on the East coast. When his uncle eventually died, he took over the business.

Deshawn was brought back to the present when Carlos spoke to him. He didn't get what was said to him the first time, because he was not paying attention, and wasn't expecting anyone to speak to him.

"What did you say Carlos?"

"I think we're being followed boss," Carlos repeated.

Deshawn was shocked when Carlos said that. He had been lost in thought about his childhood that he had not been conscious of his environment. "What makes you think so Carlos?"

"That black Chevrolet van has been following us for quite a while now."

He turned to take a look at the Chevrolet van that was behind his Mercedes. The glasses of the vehicle were tinted and he could not see the occupants of the car. However, he suspected that what Carlos said was true. Carlos had proved to be very observant, and it would be foolish to ignore the possibility of what he had just said.

He turned towards Carlos, "Don't go directly to the house. Turn left, then turn right, and then take another left, another right and another left."

"Okay, boss," Carlos responded.

Carlos carried out the instructions faithfully. Deshawn turned around to see that the van was still behind them. He was sure now that the van was trailing them. If it wasn't, it wouldn't have still being following them up till that moment. The people in the van sensed that they had been made. They increased their speed and no longer made any attempt at concealing themselves.

"Carlos, step on it!" Deshawn shouted.

Carlos slammed his foot down hard on the gas pedal and the car speedometer jerked forward. He gripped the steering wheel with both hands, as the car gradually attained a dangerous speed. His expert driving skills had earned him the nickname, The Navigator.

The speed of the van increased to match their new speed. Whoever was behind the wheels of the van was obviously no amateur and was determined to match Carlos speed for speed. Due to the other cars in front of him, Carlos could not speed up as much as he wanted. Inevitably, the black Chevrolet van started gaining on them.

Carlos braked suddenly and swerved left, the van behind them wasn't expecting the turn and so in his effort to swerve to the left too, he bumped into the rear side of the Mercedes at full speed. The force of the impact shook the occupants of both vehicles. Jamie who was sitting in the front of the vehicle, reached for the SMG that he usually kept there. He pulled it out and checked to be sure that the magazine was loaded. Carlos had also pulled out his desert eagle.

The door of the van opened, and three men in masks, wearing black jeans and long sleeve jackets, armed with assault rifles started firing at the Mercedes. Jamie reached out from the window and sprayed bullets at the advancing attackers. One of them got hit.

"Carlos what is wrong?" Deshawn yelled as he reached for his Glock 22. "Get us out of here!"

"I'm trying boss, I'm trying," Carlos said as he struggled to start the ignition. The car had refused to start, Carlos tried the ignition several times but it didn't budge, he was getting frustrated because the attackers were getting closer.

When the other two men began advancing towards the car again, Jamie fired at them again and another fell. However, they returned fire this time. Jamie was hit in the shoulder and his SMG dropped on the floor of the car. The car was riddled with bullet holes. Deshawn fired at the remaining lone attacker through the rear window of the vehicle. He missed. The attacker fired at him, he had to lay down flat on the floor of the car to avoid being hit. The glass was shattered and even the seats were hit. Just when they thought things couldn't get any worse, they saw two more men armed with machine guns, coming down from the van. Just as the two new additions got down and opened fire on the car, Carlos tried the ignition one more time and the car came to life.

Carlos slammed his foot down so hard that the tire screeched on the tarred road, releasing a bit of smoke before the car sped away. The men who had come down last from the van carried their men who had been shot back into the van. They all got in and drove off. Only one seemed to be critically hit, because the other person that was hit was helped up and into the van by one of his partners. The front part of the van looked badly damaged.

When Deshawn arrived at his house, he examined his car and found that the rear had been damaged to a large extent. His guards at home had gawked at the bullet ridden and bashed in car when they stopped at the gate so Carlos could sign in. It had been a head on collision, and the van was moving at such a high speed. He kicked the wheel of his vehicle angrily and cursed. Jamie was already being attended to by a doctor. A personal doctor that he had hired in the case of such events. Carlos was standing beside him as he vented his frustration and kicked the car tire repeatedly.

"Carlos, take care of this," he said, pointing at the Mercedes.

Carlos nodded, and he turned and went into the house. His butler was waiting with his favorite cocktail and cigar on a tray as usual. He downed the cocktail in one huge gulp, some of it running down the corners of his mouth. He didn't care, his mind was highly agitated. He ignored the cigar and climbed the stairs to his room. Once in his room, he flopped into an arm chair and wondered what the hell just happened some moments back. He didn't want to imagine what would have happened if the car had failed to start the last time that Carlos had tried to start it. It would have been the funeral of all three of them. It was nothing short of a miracle that the vehicle had started.

What bothered him was not only the fact that he had been attacked, but the fact that the attackers knew when he left the office and started trailing him. He suspected that there was a mole in his cartel. It had to be a mole because he often changed cars when he went to work so as not to be identified by the car he went in. The windows of all his vehicles were tinted and he had people who worked for him that had cars similar to his, so tracing him by depending on his vehicle would be difficult. The men that had attacked him had to be acting on reliable information from an insider. The problem that faced him now was figuring out who that intruder was and dealing with the person accordingly.

He also had to re-evaluate his decision of moving around with only one guard and Carlos. It was the first time that he had been attacked like that in broad day light, they were outnumbered, and would have probably been dead if the car did not start at the last minute. He didn't want to travel with a convoy, but at least he had to take two extra guards with him. He could not take chances.

He also considered getting a bullet proof car. He had almost been shot dead! Who knew when he was going to be attacked again. He didn't want to be caught unprepared, he had to be ready for them. He picked up his phone and dialed Sammy's number. Sammy was one of the highly placed people in his cartel and a buddy of his. He asked Sammy to get him a bullet proof car and have it delivered to him on or before the next morning. It was only after he made that call that he was able to have some relief.

His shipment was due soon and he couldn't afford for anything to go wrong. While he was still thinking about what had happened earlier that day, he got a message from Joey. Joey was the guy that was in charge of the incoming shipment. He made sure that everything went smoothly and there was no hitch. He opened the text.

Location of the shipment has been discovered. We need to change the location.

The message further convinced him that there was a mole in his organization.

The location for the exchange was out on the streets. Rival gangs could show up and try to hijack the shipment. He couldn't allow that to happen. He had initially suppressed all the other drug cartels in the city, but some of them were starting to regroup and spring up again to cause trouble. The attempt on his life might as well have been carried out by any of them. Well, he would show them who was boss.

There was a new kid in the city making waves. Don Li. He successfully took over many of the smaller cartels and was proving to be a serious threat to him. Deshawn had ignored Don Li because he had seen him as someone that was not worth his attention, but from the reports he got now, he believed it was time he reconsidered. He strongly suspected that Don Li was behind the attack on him. If he did nothing, the so called "little boy," might run him out of business one day. It was about time he took action.

That evening, he lost his appetite and couldn't eat dinner. The fact that people dared to attack him, made him mad. What nerve! He sat up in bed late into the night, thinking about who the mole in his organization was. God help that person when he caught him, he would make the person wish that he had not been born.

As he lay in bed that night, waiting for sleep to come, his mind told him why he was so angry that he almost got shot. His former self would not have minded being shot at, he knew that it was part of his line of work. The risks were high, but the rewards were higher. In the moment, when the glass of the car shattered and he lay on the floor of the vehicle, his biggest fear was that he would not get to see B'onca or his daughter again. The thought paralyzed him. When it was all over, and the attackers had retreated, he was grateful to be alive only because he knew he would see the face of his daughter and B'onca again. The thought of his kid being fatherless and B'onca not being able to provide enough for her plagued him and made him angry. That was why he had become so angry, ordered a bullet proof car and decided to use more guards.

He changed his mind again. Two additional guards were not going to be enough. He had to move with two cars. He would be in one of the cars with two guards plus Carlos, and the second car would convey four guards. That would bring their total number to six. At least with that number of people with him, he would feel safer. The only time that those guards wouldn't be with him was when he made his discreet visits to his wife and daughter. That was something no one could know about.

The fact that he was attacked made him worry more about the safety of B'onca and their daughter. Who knew if the group that had attacked him knew about their existence. One thing was obvious, the group would definitely keep coming after him, and they would most likely start shadowing him. If they discovered Britney and B'onca, they would harm them to get to him. Deshawn couldn't let that happen.

As the thoughts ran through his mind, he was overpowered by sleep. His mind shut down and he slept peacefully. He was temporarily freed from the burden of thinking about the attack on him, and who the mole in his organization could be.

CHAPTER THREE

Deshawn was usually successful in whatever he set out to do. When his uncle passed away, the business was doing well, but not as it did under him. He had expanded not only their supply chain, but a lot of things about the business. Not only did he now run the drug cartel, he also owned eight of the most popular bars in town. That too was a significant source of income to add to what he already had. The bars were spread out across the city, and he often used them as a rendezvous for meetings with members of his cartel.

After a long day of work at the office, Deshawn relaxed into the leather of the Mercedes-Maybach S650 Guard that Sammy had sent across early that morning. When he got downstairs that morning to get into his car, he was impressed with the car that Sammy had chosen. Sammy had good taste when it came to cars. He felt safer in the vehicle, at least the windows and body of the car could withstand bullets to a large extent, he only hoped that those after him did not resort to using RPG's. When he thought about the RPG part, he chuckled out loud. Carlos looked at him in the rearview mirror to know why he chuckled, but he put on a straight face. He didn't want to tell Carlos what he was thinking about. He had not yet put his plan of travelling with extra guards into action.

The car pulled into the compound of one of Deshawn's bar. The bar was the biggest of the eight bars that he owned in the city. It was starting to get dark and soon the bar would be filled with fun chasers who would be there until it was past midnight.

The white painted building was huge. Stepping in the front door brought you to the bar section that had tables with chairs around them and the usual counter with the bartenders behind it. Eight waitresses worked in that section, plus two bartenders. Then towards the left of the bar, there was a hallway that led to the club. The club section was soundproof, making it impossible for the loud music and noise to disturb those in the bar. In front of the door which led into the club, a bouncer was always stationed.

Those were the two places in the building that everyone knew of. There were many other places inside the building that was known only to the elite and gaining passage into those sections required being a member of the cartel. At the rear of the house was a mini conference room and three stores. The mini conference room was used to hold meetings, while the stores were used for storing drugs, pending transfer to the distributors. Those parts of the building were always guarded and none of the employees that worked either in the bar or in the club knew of its existence. The door that led into those places had a huge sign with "restricted area" written on it and a guard next to the door.

Tobias was standing next to Deshawn's vehicle when he stepped out. Tobias's eyes shone with admiration at the new wheels in front of him. Tobias looked so much like his twin brother Carlos. They both had short curly brown hair, and a South American accent. They were almost the same height, and it was easy for someone meeting them for the first time, to get confused about who was who. Tobias had always dreamt of getting something like that for himself. He loved German cars, especially the ones that were armored. It was his first time seeing the vehicle since it was bought the previous night.

"Good evening, boss. Shiny new ride you've got there," he said.

Deshawn smiled and looked at the vehicle. He nodded in agreement. The car was a real peach. He only hoped that he didn't have to buy an armored tank next to protect himself. He laughed inwardly at the thought.

"Yeah Tobias, she's a good one." Deshawn turned again towards Tobias and gesticulated towards the building, "Has everyone arrived?"

"Yes, except Leo and Tom."

Deshawn nodded. He was making his way into the building when a red Lexus drove into the premises. He paused in his tracks, he knew it was Tom driving in. He was the only one who drove a red Lexus in his cartel. The vehicle parked and Tom climbed out. Tom was the guy in charge of all distribution. It was his duty to distribute the drugs to other distributors or sellers. It was also his duty to ensure that every dollar was accounted for. Tom used to be an accountant with a bank, before he started working for

Deshawn, and then resigned. He walked up to Deshawn smiling.

"Good evening Shawn. I hope I didn't miss the party?"

"Just in time," Deshawn said.

He wondered why Leo hadn't showed up yet. Leo had been notified early enough about the meeting. He was also a high ranked member of the cartel who was supposed to be at the meeting. Deshawn swallowed the anger that was rising in him as he and Tom made their way into the building. The guard at the entrance of the door that led to the mini conference room nodded his greeting as they walked past him and into the room where the meeting was to be held.

There were four chairs on an elevated platform in the room where Deshawn and his three lieutenants usually sat while the other chairs were arranged in a semi-circle in front of them. The others were already seated when Deshawn came in with Tom at his heel and Tobias behind them. Sammy was sitting on one of the four chairs in the front of the room. Tom took the next seat beside Sammy, while Deshawn sat next to him. The other vacant seat was for Leo, but he did not show up. Sammy handed Deshawn a bunch of papers which he leafed through for a moment without saying anything. There was pin drop silence in the room.

On the chairs facing the elevated platform, Tobias, Stefan, Gary and six other guys were seated. They had all arrived before Deshawn and had been sitting there waiting for him. Now that he was in the room, they waited for him to finish what he was looking at and tell them exactly what the meeting was for. They sat with expectant looks on their faces.

Finally, when Deshawn was finished leafing through the papers handed to him, he dropped them on the vacant seat next to him. He cleared his throat before he began, "I have received information from reliable sources that there are plans to sabotage the shipment coming in tonight. It is imperative that we move the exchange to a new location. From the information that I have received, the one planning this attack is no other person than Don Li. Yes, Don Li, the new kid on the block. It's no longer news that he has been trying to take control of supply in the areas that we currently control. It is also he who has been sabotaging our previous smaller shipments. And I know that he has also been trying to convince some members of this organization to join him."

Deshawn paused for effect, he scanned the faces of the people in the room. Their eyes were fixed upon him. He stepped down from the elevated platform and continued his speech. "However, I have come up with a plan to counter the planned attack. Sammy will take some men to the new delivery location, which he has already set up with the suppliers. Tobias will take another group of men to meet Don Li's men at the original location. I have had enough of his crap, it's time we sent a message across to him. Tobias, you and your men are to take the armored van. I want you to hit them as hard as you can, that will teach them not to mess with us next time."

Tobias looked at him and nodded to show that he understood what he was instructed to do. Deshawn nodded in his direction too.

"Now, on to something else that is just as important," Deshawn continued. "I think there is a mole within this organization." He paused to see the effect that his words had on his audience. They each had that look of shock and surprise written on it. He looked from one to another, searching their faces. He had hoped that when he said that, maybe the mole's facial expression would give him away, but he couldn't come to any conclusion from the facial expressions of the men in front of him. He was quite convinced that there was a mole in his cartel, and he was going to fish the person out, whoever it was, it would only take time.

"Some of you may not know it, but I was attacked yesterday. The attackers shot at my car and hit Jamie in the shoulder, he is receiving treatment as we speak. This is something that has never happened before, and I am convinced that the attackers were informed about my movement by an insider. I also have reasons to believe that it is the same person who planned the attack on me, that keeps sabotaging my shipments. However, I have decided to be magnanimous. If the person will come forward and confess to me, his punishment shall be lighter, but if he leaves me to fish him out myself, the consequences will be grave."

He looked around the room, there was no movement. "Alright," he said. "We all meet at safe house number two when the deal is done and when you've finished your business with Don Li's men. Everyone should be at the safe house by 20:00 at the latest. And I'd like a detailed report of how everything goes. That'll be all gentlemen."

When he said that, they all rose from their seats and started leaving the room one after the other. He was the last to leave the room, and he took the papers that Sammy had given him along. He took a look at his wristwatch as soon as he stepped outside into the open space, it was almost 7pm. The exchange was scheduled to happen by 8:30pm. He could only hope that everything went smoothly.

Carlos was standing by his vehicle when he came out. Carlos wasn't included in such meetings, his job was to drive Deshawn around and act as his bodyguard if the need arose. He walked towards the car, Carlos opened the door for him and he got in. When Carlos had gotten into the car and was seated in the driver's seat, Deshawn said to him, "To the safe house."

Carlos nodded his head and started the ignition. He tuned to a channel that was playing country music, and nodded his head to the music as he drove, drumming on the steering wheel with his fingers. Deshawn wished that he could be free and vibe to the song, but he couldn't. He was apprehensive about the deal that was going down that night. He couldn't be settled or relaxed – not until he received a success report. The deal was a big one.

Carlos pulled into the underground parking lot of the safe house. There were a few cars parked there that Deshawn couldn't recognize. He wondered who owned the cars and what they were doing there. He got down from his car as soon as it came to a halt. He walked to the door of the safe house that connected with the underground parking lot, all was quiet. The quietness unsettled him. Carlos was a few steps behind him. He pulled his gun and cocked it, Carlos likewise pulled his weapon. Carlos cast him a questioning look. He placed a hand across his lips to tell Carlos to shut up, then he whispered, "I think there is something wrong." Carlos nodded in agreement to what he said.

Deshawn opened the door, and slowly went up the steps with Carlos behind him. When they finished ascending the second flight of stairs, he could hear some noise, he couldn't decipher what it was at the moment. On drawing closer, his brain identified the sound, it was music. But wait, who would be at the safe house playing music at that time. He didn't let his guard down just yet. He still advanced slowly towards the sound of the music. When he finally opened the door that led into the safe house proper, he saw people dancing with glasses of drinks in their hands. The music was very loud, and the people inside moved their body to the beat.

The whole place stank of alcohol. There were tables in the room laden with coke and drinks from beer to vodka or whiskey. On some of the sofas in the room, men and women were bent over the tables in front of them, snorting. Some of them were already wasted, and quite a number of them were drunk. Many of them were already getting up to naughty behaviors. In the right corner of the room, a man and a woman were kissing. The woman's breasts had been released from their confinement, and the man had his hands on them, squeezing them like his life depended on it. Though he could not hear it because of the loud music, from the way the woman's lips were parted, he could tell that she was moaning. One of the man's hands descended from her bare breast, and started making its way into her parted thighs.

"What the fuck," Deshawn said, as his gun dropped to his side. What in the hell was happening in the safe house. Who permitted these people to come in here, and do as they please. Carlos came in and stood beside him with the same look of surprise on his face. Deshawn glanced around the place to know if he could recognize any of them, but he couldn't. He moved into the room further before he spotted Leo laughing with a group of people. They all had glasses in their hands. Carlos was closely behind him the whole time. He moved to Leo and tapped him hard on his shoulder, Leo looked surprised to see him. He made the come-hither movement with his hand and headed towards his office at the back.

Leo was a member of Deshawn's gang, and a high ranking one at that. He was an Asian American. He had jet straight, black hair that spoke of his Asian ancestry. But his face did not look so much like a typical Asian's. He had blue eyes and long black lashes. His nose was straight and rounded beautifully at the tip. He had small red lips that often made women stare. He was quite the ladies' man, coupled with his impressive height of nearly six feet. He was the type of man that any lady would easily be attracted to physically.

Leo excused himself and followed Deshawn. Carlos was behind them. The office that they entered was a small one, the large table and the two seats in it took up most of the space in the room. There was barely enough room for three people that were standing. It looked like the office had been put there as an afterthought and was not originally included in the plan of the place. There were files on the table piled upon one another. It seemed the whole thing would come crashing down if one more file was added on top. The room smelt like something that was not used too often. On the ceiling of the room, a fan was hanging down, with the control box on the wall next to the door. The furniture looked dusty, so nobody bothered to sit. Not like any of them were in the mood for sitting.

When all three were in the room, Deshawn turned to Carlos. "Could you please give us a moment alone?"

Carlos looked from one to the other, before he stuck his hands in his pocket and said, "Sure." He then turned and walked out of the room. He stood in the passageway that led to the room, quite a distance from the door.

As soon as Carlos was out of the room, Deshawn grabbed Leo roughly by the collar. "What the hell do you think you're doing? Of all the days to party, why today?"

"Take it easy man, you're hurting me," Leo said, and winced in pain.

"I'm going to hurt you even more if you don't explain why you were absent from the meeting?"

"The meeting? It was today? I thought it was tomorrow."

Deshawn looked at Leo and felt like hitting him across the face. How could he give such a flimsy excuse for missing a meeting that he was notified about? Leo had never been the type that took anything too seriously, he only managed to rise in the ranks because he always brought innovative ideas about how they could bypass security checks in transporting their drugs.

"You thought?" Deshawn asked, unable to disguise his irritation.

"Yeah, I got the text. But, I miscalculated the date and thought that the twenty-sixth was tomorrow, I didn't know it was today."

Deshawn looked at him, the temptation of hitting him rose with each word he uttered. If it had been someone else, someone that was a lower ranking member, he would have hit the person long ago. "So, what are you doing? Getting high on drugs? Don't you know the number one rule of this business? Never get high on your own supply."

Deshawn knew how dangerous it was to get high on drugs that you were selling. Anything and everything could go wrong if that happened. He didn't want to take chances and Leo bringing in people that he didn't know to the safe house? That was a whole new level of disrespect.

"I swear Shawn, I wasn't getting high on any drugs," Leo said. "It's only my friends who came for the party that were getting high. I promise you that all those drugs can be accounted for to the last dollar."

When he said that, Deshawn lessened his grip on his collar, and finally released his hold on him. He was at least somewhat glad that his merchandise was not being used to entertain the guests for free. Leo had the common sense to make sure that he had the payment for them. But, he still wasn't happy that Leo had brought his guests to the safe house for a party. A safe house was supposed to be a secret location, known to only members for whom it was intended. He didn't in any way approve of Leo's irresponsible act.

"Why did you invite all these people here to party?"

"I was just feeling bored and wanted to have a little fun," Leo said.

"That's why you threw a party in a safe house? This is a safe house for God's sake Leo. A safe house!"

"I'm sorry about that, I guess I didn't really think it through."

" I don't even know those people that you invited in here. Any of them could be a spy for all I know."

Leo kept mute and stared at the floor in front of him. He looked remorseful, like a schoolboy being scolded by his teacher.

"I need you to clear that lounge out in the next twenty minutes. Tobias and the rest are coming."

Leo nodded and left the room. He was only too happy to leave and carry out the instructions given to him. When Carlos saw Leo come out of the office, he went in. When he entered, Deshawn was standing next to the table in the room, dusting it with a rag. When he was done with the table, he started on the chairs. Carlos stood next to the doorway, watching him.

Tobias was waiting with eight men at the location where the exchange was to have taken place. They had been there for quite a long time, waiting for Don Li's men to arrive. This was the showdown, it was time to hit back at Don Li who had caused them so much trouble. Tobias glanced at his watch for the seventh time that hour, it was almost eight thirty, they had been waiting for close to one hour at the spot.

The location was a junk yard filled with disused cars. Cars that had no tires, windshields, or anything else for that matter littered the whole yard. Some of the cars that had become nothing more than scraps were placed atop one another. Tobias had some of his men hide behind some of the cars, while some stood with him. Finally, it was eight thirty, nothing happened. Eight thirty-three, and still nothing.

Then, all of a sudden, a Toyota car came in their direction at full speed. Tobias and the three men standing with him had to dive out of the way to avoid getting hit by the oncoming vehicle. The vehicle was still in motion when the occupants jumped out and opened fire on Tobias and the men with him. Tobias ducked next to a car and fired at the men that got out of the vehicle.

One of the men that had been standing with Tobias was gunned down immediately. From his cover, Tobias shot two of the men that had alighted from the Toyota. There were about seven men in total, plus the driver. The men from Don Li's side were outnumbered. Initially, Deshawn wouldn't have dispatched as much as nine men to the delivery point. He would have deployed a maximum of five, but because he knew that they were expecting company, he had to make sure that there were enough men to hit back at Don Li's men.

Don Li's men spread out, some of them hiding next to the abandoned cars. Deshawn's men who were hidden began firing at them. The gun duel was fierce. One of Deshawn's men attempted to advance further towards the enemy and was shot in the chest. The other men with Tobias kept firing at Don Li's men, without letting up. Don Li's men soon realized that they had been lured into a trap and it would be difficult to escape, but they had to at least try, if not they would all become toast. They started moving back towards the vehicle to make a gateway, in the process of trying to get into the vehicle, another two of Don Li's men got shot. The remaining two got into the car, and the driver sped off.

When the men had gone, Deshawn's men carried their own men that had been shot and put them in the back of their van. They drove off towards the direction of the safe house. Deshawn was waiting for them to come and give him a report about how everything went.

Tobias and his men were the last group to arrive to the safe house. By the time they arrived, Deshawn couldn't resist the urge to party. He had already opened bottles of wine, and poured some for everyone. He was elated that the exchange had gone so smoothly, he had been worried that something would go wrong, and he couldn't contain his excitement when everything finally turned out right in the end. Everyone was seated in the lounge, glass in hand when Tobias and the remaining six men came in.

"Tobias, welcome to the party," Deshawn beamed. However, Deshawn quickly observed that Tobias didn't return his smile, and that he wore a sad look. Deshawn asked, "Did anything go wrong?"

"Nothing really went wrong, we were able to hit Don Li's men hard, but we lost two men. Tyler and Chris."

"Two men," Deshawn said slowly, like he was thinking about something. "How many of their men did you kill?"

"Four boss, before they finally escaped in their car."

Deshawn turned sober, he dropped the glass of wine in his hand on the table. Nobody was drinking anymore, everyone just held their glasses in their hand rocking it back and forth, or they set it down on the floor. Deshawn felt bad that they had lost men, he didn't want that to happen. He had hoped that all his men would somehow come back alive. Though he had one consolation from the whole incident. Don Li would think twice about it before trying to sabotage any of his deals again. Four men in one day was a big loss to any cartel. He had to think up a more decisive way to deal with Don Li once and for all. Enough was enough.

He turned towards Tobias, "Bury the dead." He gestured towards Tobias and the men that came in with him, "You guys can drink too if you want," he said, and pointed at the bottles and glasses on the table. "I need to get home and rest."

Carlos stood up immediately when Deshawn mentioned home. He set his glass of unfinished wine down on the table and followed Deshawn as he made his way out. Stefan also stood, and followed them. When Deshawn passed Tobias, he tapped his shoulder twice, saying, "You did your best. Don't blame yourself for their deaths."

Deshawn walked down the steps slowly and Carlos got the car door for him as usual. Stefan got into the front seat. He was going to be the interim replacement for Jamie, until he recovered enough to resume work. Deshawn decided that he would implement his idea of extra security the next day. He couldn't delay any further, who knew what the son of a bitch Don Li was planning. The ride home was quiet, nobody said anything, and Carlos did not play any music in the car. They all kept mute until Carlos pulled up in front of the door of Deshawn's mansion. Deshawn and Stefan slighted from the car, while Carlos took the car to the parking lot. Once inside the house, Stefan headed for the room where he was to pass the night and bade Deshawn goodnight.

The butler, as usual, presented a glass of Deshawn's favorite cocktail to him but for the first time in a long time, he declined. He had a lot to think about, and he certainly wasn't in the mood for any drink. Don Li was actually become a pain in the ass more than he ever imagined was possible. The attack that night was not enough, he knew Don Li would try to take revenge. He had to think of a more concrete plan to get rid of Don Li for good.

As he changed his clothes he felt like he needed a shower, but he wasn't quite in the mood to do anything. It was not the first time that he has los men to gang wars, though this one saddened him because Tyler was a lad that he loved. He had big plans for him. Tyler was one of the boys that you could trust to see an errand to its end. He was always on time and he always did as he was told without asking questions. Now, all of a sudden, he's gone.

Delivery within the neighborhoods that he controlled had been going peacefully for quite a long time. Then, one day, Don Li came into the picture and started selling in some of his neighborhoods. His men had clashed several times with Don Li's men on the streets, in a bid to control neighborhood supplies.

He hadn't really taken Don Li as a serious threat then, he had just seen him as a little lad trying to make a couple of bucks. But then, Don Li started sabotaging his shipments and trying to get his men to join his own cartel. And now, Don Li had risen to the level of even trying to sabotage one of his biggest shipments, and make an attempt on his life. He knew that he had quite a lot of enemies, but he could swear that Don Li was the one who had sent men after him. Well, tonight's hit was only the beginning. He was still going to hit him harder.

He would think up a plan to that effect. First, he would destabilize his men that ran supplies for him. That was the first step, before his men finished carrying that out, he would have thought up another plan. He also thought it high time he returned Don Li's favor of attacking him on his way home. But, he wanted to bid his time. The timing was not right yet, he would strike when it was, and by God, Don Li wouldn't be able to escape from him. He would trap him like the little mouse that he was and squash him with his foot.

He got into bed without taking his shower and rested his head on the pillow. He grabbed his phone and texted Sammy, asking him to make available another bullet proof vehicle and four men the next morning. Now that things were starting to get hotter, he might as well tighten his security. It was only after he had put that in place that he was able to sleep. His sleep was, however, a fitful one.

CHAPTER FOUR

A few days after the shipment of drugs arrived, Deshawn was in one of his safe houses going through paperwork with a glass of wine beside him. He had been sitting there for a while, flipping through the pages of the document he held. He heard the door open and close, then Sammy appeared pulling a young man by his collar. He shoved the young man to the ground in front of Deshawn and held a gun to his head.

"What is the matter Sammy?" Deshawn asked.

"This little bastard here is one of Don Li's men. We had seen him earlier hanging out with his gang and later today he had the nerve to walk up to a group of our men. He kept saying that he wanted to speak to you and that he would not speak to anyone else, so I bundled him here."

Deshawn rose from his sitting position and walked up to the young man, who looked more like a kid. "What's your business here boy? I believe you work for Don Li, so what are you doing snooping around?"

The young man stood up brushing off nonexistent dust from his clothes. He looked nervous, and the fact that Sammy still had a gun pointed at him didn't seem to help matters at all. Deshawn signaled to Sammy to lower the gun. It was only then that the young man composed himself a bit and was able to speak. "My name is Jimmy, my cousin works for Don Li. I happened to overhear their plans to attack the warehouse where your last shipment was put in, so I came to warn you and your men."

"Go on," Deshawn said.

"I want to be part of your crew. I ran a couple of drug deliveries for Don Li, but he didn't pay me well like he should have. I just need money to pay for my mother's cancer treatments. I promise to pay back or I can work for you for free to work off my debt. I will do anything just to get this money. My mother is dying, and I need to save her. Somehow Don Li knows the location of the warehouse where the last shipment that came in was put. But, one thing I know, Don Li plans to break into it tonight and clear the place out."

Deshawn was not so surprised by the information. He already knew that there was a mole within his ranks that kept sabotaging his operations. His biggest problem was identifying who the person was and dealing with him accordingly. What he would do to the person when he finally caught him, even the devil would reject his soul in hell.

"Jimmy, my boy, you're a good lad. My instincts tell me that what you say is true, but in this business you don't rely solely on your instincts. I have to verify the information that you gave me and if turns out to be correct you will definitely be rewarded. But, if it turns out to be false, well, I can't say."

Deshawn signals Sammy to grab Jimmy and Sammy does so, roughly and by the collar. "Sammy," Deshawn said reproachfully, "That's not how you treat a guest, where are your manners. Handle him better."

Sammy lessened his grip on Jimmy's collar. "Much better," Deshawn said.

"Now, my lad," he said to Jimmy. "I hope you don't mind being locked up for a couple of hours while I go verify the information that you gave me?"

Jimmy nodded in the affirmative.

"That's a good lad. Sammy please show our guest to where he will be spending the next couple of hours."

Sammy led Jimmy down a dark passage, and pushed open a door on the left. He pushed Jimmy in and locked the door. Jimmy looked around the place, the room was lit by a single yellow bulb, there was a chair inside the room and a desk. He wiped the desk with his handkerchief and sat on it. The room smelt like an abandoned place, somewhere that people did not go into often. The furniture in the room was dusty and he could see low hanging cobwebs at the edges of the ceiling. Of all the places to lock him in, why in this God forsaken place? he thought to himself. The door opened again, and Sammy came in. He was holding a bottle of water and a bag of chips. He dropped them on the table and then went out again, locking the door after him.

When Sammy rejoined Deshawn, he was on the phone. "Yes, bring Stefan along with you on your way here." He ended the call.

"Who were you calling?"

"Tobias. I asked him to come over here and also bring Stefan with him. We have to move the shipment to a different warehouse ASAP." Sammy nodded.

As Deshawn waited for Tobias and Stefan, he paced up and down. Don Li never seemed to take a break. Just a few days ago, he had lost four men in a bid to hijack his shipment. He had thought that would keep him off for quite a while, but no. In a matter of days, Don Li had organized again, to hit his warehouse and clear it out. If not for the warning by Jimmy, Don Li would have caught him off guard because he wasn't expecting him back so soon. Though the information he received had not been verified, he knew it was true. Don Li was a son of a bitch who had somehow managed to win one of his men over.

After that night, he planned to strike back at Don Li. To hit him as hard as possible. Don Li had been the one making the moves and he had been in the defense all along. That was about to change. He was going to attack first from now on, he wouldn't give Don Li the chance to get up to any pretty little ideas anymore. He would keep him busy and on his toes, and if he got the chance, he would take Don Li out once and for all. He had taken enough of his crap.

As he was still pacing the room, Tobias and Stefan arrived. Sammy was sitting and thinking while Deshawn paced. Tobias and Stefan greeted him but he didn't respond. He merely nodded and then waved them to a seat. He wasn't in the mood for exchange of greetings. A serious matter had brought them there and they were going to go straight to the matter at hand.

"Gentlemen, we have a serious matter," Deshawn said as soon as the latest arrivals were seated. "Don Li is up to it again. I have received information that he will attack the warehouse where the last shipment was stored, and clear it out. However, we cannot let that happen. We have to act fast. The shipment has to be moved earlier this evening, before night time which I gather they plan to strike. Stefan and Tobias, you will lead a team of men to move the shipment. Afterwards, head back to the original warehouse where the shipment was stored and wait for Don Li's men."

Deshawn paused his speech and looked at the three men seated before him, he wondered if one of them was the mole that was always leaking information to Don Li. He trusted them, but recent events have caused him to question everyone around him. He didn't seem to know who to trust these days. "Any questions?" he asked.

None of them spoke.

"That'll be all for now gentlemen."

Tobias and Stefan stood up and started heading towards the door. Sammy was still seated where he was. Stefan went out first and when Tobias's hand was on the door handle Deshawn called out to him, "Tobias, bring the boys home this time."

Tobias paused for a moment, then nodded and went out.

Deshawn slumped into the seat next to Sammy. He felt like drinking to calm himself down. The fact that his men were going to have another encounter with Don Li's men somehow unsettled him. He didn't want to lose anyone again, especially one of the upcoming lads with great potential. He decided against drinking, instead he would go home. He got up and tapped Sammy on the shoulder, before heading out.

When he got to the parking lot, Carlos and Jamie were standing beside the car. Jamie had recovered and resumed duty immediately. There were five other men there besides Carlos and Jamie. Some were in the black Mercedes Benz S600 Guard parked beside the Mercedes-Maybach S650 Guard, while some were standing around leaning on the cars. When Deshawn got closer, Carlos in his usual way got the door for him. Carlos got behind the wheel, with Jamie in the front and a guard got in the back next to Deshawn.

"Where to boss?" Carlos asked.

"Home."

Carlos started the ignition and headed out of the parking lot, followed behind by the other car. Deshawn still had that feeling of uneasiness in his belly as Carlos drove towards his house. Sometimes he wished he could go out with the boys and see for himself how things went, and also ensure that nothing went wrong. Well, he had no choice but to wait, he would get feedback when everything was over.

****

Tobias and Stefan led an extra twelve men to the warehouse where the shipment had been stored to transfer it to another warehouse. The men who guarded the warehouse were surprised about the sudden move that no one informed them about. Deshawn's men arrived to the warehouse in two black vans with tinted glasses, seven men per van. They all got down and transferred the shipment from the warehouse into the two vans. When they were done, Tobias stationed ten of the men to remain there while two accompanied him and Stefan to the new location. Stefan drove one of the vans with a guard sitting beside him in front, likewise Tobias.

After changing the location of the shipment, Tobias and Stefan returned with the men to the warehouse where their men were waiting. Tobias laid out an attack formation. He had made sure he brought a large number of men, so that Don Li's men would be hit from all sides, and heavy casualties would be inflicted on them. He stationed the men in several parts of the warehouse, and the compound. Then they waited patiently.

Tobias was standing next to Stefan as they waited. "You nervous?" Stefan asked.

"A little bit," Tobias replied.

Stefan pulled chewing gum from his breast pocket. He unwrapped it and threw it into his mouth. "Want one?"

"Yeah, sure."

Stefan handed him a piece. They chewed silently, waiting. The gum provided some distraction.

Soon enough a van drove into the warehouse at top speed, beaming its headlights. The van swerved dangerously to the right, and someone from the van threw a flash bang. As it exploded, the men in the van slighted, firing at Deshawn's men guarding the warehouse.

Deshawn's men returned fire, taking cover behind their vehicles. Five men had alighted from the van. As the shooting went on, one of Don Li's men got shot in the head. Stefan was firing at one of the men, when he ran out of bullets in his mag. When he took cover to reload, the man he had been shooting at advanced to take him out. Unknown to the man, Tobias was positioned behind a van to the right of Stefan. As the man moved in, Tobias shot him three times in the back before he even got the chance to turn. Stefan nodded his thanks and then resumed shooting at the other attackers.

As the gun fight continued, another car came speeding in with back up for Don Li's men. The car parked and four other men got out. As soon as they came down from the car, some of Deshawn's men who were positioned at one of the vans parked near the gate began to move in and gunned down two of the men as they stepped down from the car.

Don Li's men noticed that they were taking heavy casualties and decided to retreat. One of them got behind the wheel of the van. Another scrambled into the van and the third person, in his attempt to get in, was shot. The van screeched off in reverse at full speed. When the van was about to leave the premises, a driver stationed in one of Deshawn's van's close to the gate rammed into the front. Two of Deshawn's men near the exit moved in to finish off the occupants of the damaged van, but when they got to the front of the vehicle, the driver and his companion were lying unconscious with blood streaming down the sides of their faces. Deshawn's men shot them in the head nonetheless, to ensure that their ghosts stayed dead.

The two remaining men from Don Li's gang managed to get into the second car that they had come in. The driver revved the engine hard. He reversed swiftly and sped towards the exit. The men that were close to the warehouse fired at the vehicle as it reversed while the men who had been stationed close to the exit also shot at it. The car made its way out, but it was all in vain because the car was bullet proof. The car and its occupants escaped to safety.

"Damn it," Tobias said, frustrated that the two guys had escaped.

"Don't worry, at least they'll deliver the message to their boss," Stefan said, patting Tobias on the shoulder.

Everyone on their team was okay. Some sustained minor bruises and cuts during the shooting, but everyone was fine.

They parked the damaged van closer to the warehouse, pending when it would be towed to the repair shop. Someone was stationed across the street from the warehouse to watch it in case anyone went in there. The rest of the men got into the other vans and as they drove away from the warehouse Tobias whipped out his phone and began to type a text

Deshawn was in bed. He had been there for close to an hour, waiting for sleep. But, the sleep refused to come. He was expecting news. Until he received the news he knew that he wouldn't be able to sleep. His phone buzzed and he looked at it. There was a message from Tobias. He picked up the phone, and opened the message. It was composed of three lines: *Job done. Seven men down. No casualties.*

Deshawn smiled when he saw the message. Don Li was finally getting the pay back that he deserved. The loss of seven of his men was sure to destabilize him. Don Li had lost eleven men in a matter of days, that would definitely cool him off. He would need some time to recruit and strategize. While Don Li was still trying to find his bearings, he would strike. It was the perfect moment for him. Don Li wouldn't be expecting him. Don Li would believe that he would be basking in the euphoria of his two recent victories. But, in that moment when he wasn't expected, he would strike. As much as Don Li had not gotten the better of him in their recent clashes, he had always been on the defensive. Don Li had always been the one attacking. It was time he switched to the offensive.

He closed his eyes. He was already formulating a plan in his head that was taking a concrete form. He decided to stop thinking about the plan and get some sleep, the next day was going to be a busy one.

——— ——— ———

Jimmy woke up to find light coming in through the door and Deshawn standing in the framed doorway. He had a smile on his face. He pushed his hands into his pocket, and advanced into the room. Stefan followed closely behind.

"Jimmy, my boy," Deshawn said. "How are you this morning?"

Jimmy rose from the table where he had passed the night. His joints felt stiff. His body felt like someone had attacked him the previous night with a club. He stretched himself like a tired dog, and his joints creaked.

"I can see you are doing fine," Deshawn continued with a smile.

Jimmy didn't say anything. He sat on the table, looking at Deshawn and wondering why he was smiling so much. The empty plastic water bottle, and the wrapper of the chips were on the floor.

"Jimmy, my boy, the information you gave me about Don Li was correct. It really helped me a great deal and I must tell you that I am grateful. I am a man who rewards every kind act like yours. But then, I hate it when people try to get smart with me."

Jimmy finally understood the reason why Deshawn had been beaming smiles at him all along, his tip off had proved to be useful.

"Please come with me to the lounge, Jimmy," Deshawn said, gesturing towards the door.

Jimmy climbed down from the table following Deshawn out of the room and into the passage that led to the lounge. When they got there, there was a bottle of drink on the table and Sammy was sitting on one of the sofas. Deshawn waved him to a seat and he sat down, though wasn't comfortable because Stefan was hovering around him.

Deshawn observed what was going on, "Stefan, please give our guest some space. Take a seat or come and stand beside me if you must."

Stefan moved away from Jimmy and closer to where Deshawn and Sammy were sitting. Jimmy looked visibly relieved when he moved away. It was obvious that his presence had been causing the young man much discomfort.

"Now, Jimmy, like I was saying earlier," Deshawn continued. "I am grateful for the information that you provided me. It really helped me a lot. And for that, I am going to help you. You said you need money for your mother's cancer treatments?"

"Yes," Jimmy said.

"How much do you need?"

"Twenty grand should do."

"Done," Deshawn said. He motioned to Sammy who was sitting beside him. Sammy stood up and moved to where Jimmy was sitting and handed him a huge brown envelope. Jimmy opened the envelope and looked into it, he then wrapped it up again.

"In there, is thirty thousand dollars. I have decided to give you the loan so that you can help your mother. You can also come and work for me, that is if you want to. However, Jimmy, you do have a time frame to pay me back. You have four months to get my money back to me. I hope I am clear?"

"Yes."

"Good. Now that we understand ourselves, that is settled. You can pour yourself some wine, if you care."

"No thank you, I am fine. Can I go now?"

"Sure, why not," Deshawn said. "Stefan please, see our guest off." He turned back to Jimmy who was already standing and ready to leave. "Would you like a ride home Jimmy? I can arrange that."

"Thanks, but I can find my way home."

"That's some cash you've got there, are you sure you don't want a ride home?"

"I'm sure, thank you."

Jimmy turned and started to walk towards the door. Stefan followed behind him.

"Shawn, are you sure you're not making a mistake?" Sammy asked, turning to Deshawn.

"How?"

"By loaning the kid such an amount of money."

Deshawn chuckled. He understood what Sammy was trying to say. "Sammy, that is our way of showing gratitude. The kid really did us a good turn."

"We could have just given him a couple of thousands for his trouble. What if he isn't able to pay back?"

"That shouldn't be a problem in any way," Deshawn said. "I offered him the opportunity of working for me, don't you remember? If he is unable to raise the funds, he also has the option of working if off."

Sammy didn't look convinced. He shrugged his shoulders. "So, you're really serious about hiring him?"

"Sure, why not?"

"You think you can trust him? He just snitched on his own boss."

"Yes, I have a good feeling about him. Never mind the fact that he ratted Don Li out."

"If you say so," Sammy said, with a note of resignation in his voice.

"I say so Sammy," Deshawn said. "And if you don't mind, I'll excuse myself. I have to head over to the office now."

Deshawn went outside the house to where Carlos and the boys were waiting for him. He got into the car and instructed Carlos to take him to the office.

Deshawn didn't spend as much time in the office as he usually did. There was work, but it wasn't too much, and besides he couldn't concentrate. Several issues were on his mind. He did as much work as he could manage to do, before he sat down in his office to rest for a while. He concluded that he had done enough for one day. He packed up, locked his office and headed downstairs.

While the car sped on towards home, Deshawn wondered if Sammy was right. Maybe he had trusted Jimmy too easily. The fact that Jimmy had given him information that helped him repel Don Li's men was not enough reason to trust him blindly. Did he make a mistake loaning Jimmy that huge sum of money? All these questions swarmed in his mind, and he searched for answers to them. Someone that betrayed his boss wasn't someone that should be trusted easily, maybe he should have waited a bit, until Jimmy had proven that he could be trusted. Well, time would tell whether his instincts had been right or wrong.

Other thoughts apart from Jimmy and Don Li plagued him. Britney's birthday was around the corner. He had never attended any of her birthday parties. He was either too busy to make out the time to attend or he was scared that he would be followed if he attended the party. He always sent her gifts through B'onca, but he felt the need to attend her fourth birthday party this year. He felt that his daughter was growing up without really knowing him and they never bonded. His conscience repeatedly told him that he was becoming a worse father than his own father had been. That was something he considered unacceptable, because he rated his father as a bad father by all standards.

Apart from going over to B'onca's house because of their daughter's birthday ceremony, he also wanted to see B'onca. It had been quite a while since he saw her last. Sometimes the way he longed to go and see her and their child trouble him. All through his life, he had never felt that kind of attraction to someone. It was unexplainable. When he calculated the risks involved with going over to see B'onca and their daughter, the risk of being caught, it made him keep away from them. But, he never managed to keep away for too long. The longing that he felt was not just a surface longing for something that he wanted, it was like a core need that had to be met. As demanding as the need to eat, drink or sleep. It was a need that often took him all of his self-control to resist. Many times, he didn't manage to resist it successfully and therefore caved in.

Deshawn was lost in thought, he only became aware of his surroundings when Carlos opened the door to let him out of the car. He wasn't aware when they got to the house or when Carlos cut the ignition. As he stepped out of the car, he chided himself. He had to do better. He was getting absent minded too often and that wasn't good. In his line of work, one had to be alert always. He got down from the vehicle and nodded at Carlos.

As he ate dinner that night, one thing was clear to him. He was becoming too attached to his family, and sooner or later, one of his numerous enemies were going to use it against him. The last thing that he wanted was any harm befalling B'onca or his daughter. Though he had increased the frequency of his visits to them, B'onca still complained that it was not enough and that he often came by when their daughter was already asleep. They were both innocent and ignorant of what he did for a living. They knew nothing of his numerous enemies or that he rarely came to their house as a way to protect them.

He finished dinner and dragged himself up to his room. He thought about what would be the perfect birthday present for his daughter as he got into bed. He didn't know what a four-year-old girl would love most. He decided not to let that bother him, he would know how to cross that bridge when he got to it.

CHAPTER FIVE

Deshawn woke up feeling a strange kind of excitement though he didn't know what made him excited. He got up from his bed and stretched then it hit him. The next day was his daughter's birthday. He didn't know why he felt excited about it, he felt that it wasn't something that should excite him since he had no plans of attending her birthday party. However, when he went into the bathroom to have a shower, and afterwards while he dressed, he was thinking about the issue. He knew that he wasn't supposed to go, that their safety depended on his ability to keep away from them. However, he felt a strange urge to go and see B'onca and his daughter.

Many times, Deshawn wished things weren't the way they were. He wished he could change some aspects of his life. Many days, he felt a strange emptiness and deep longing within him. On those days, all he wanted to do was abandon everything else, and be with his family. But then, the fear of someone following him and bringing harm to the two people he cared most for, always kept him away He wished he didn't have to live with that fear, but this was the life he had signed up for. He had to face it.

On other days, the longing to see B'onca and his child would be replaced by anger. He would get angry with himself and wonder how he had let his guard down and allowed a woman into his life. How could he have been so reckless? How could he be so stupid? He knew the kind of work that he did and he knew that in his line of work, people that you cared for could always be used against you.

To add to his worries, they had a daughter. A daughter who made him, for the first time in his life, question his lifestyle and motives. All his life, he had always been sure of himself. He had always known what he wanted and had gone for it. But now, he wasn't sure what he wanted anymore. He felt weak and vulnerable. He often wondered how two people that he had known for less than ten years came to wield such power over him. He didn't even spend much time with them, and yet they had a hold on his heart that no one else ever had.

When he got to the office, he couldn't concentrate on his work. He kept getting distracted. He would have left the office earlier, there was too much work to be done. The recent issues with his last shipment had taken up most of his time, leaving most of his other duties unattended to. Now that those issues were out of the way, he had to catch up on all the work that had piled up during the period. In his bid to work as much as he could, to reduce the accumulated work, he lost track of time. He was shocked when he looked at his wristwatch and discovered it was past six. He remembered he had yet to buy a birthday present for his daughter. He promptly packed up, and left.

When Deshawn got to the parking lot, he encountered another problem that he had not really given thought to. Five of his guards, plus Carlos were waiting for him next to the cars. He wanted to head over to the toy store and get some stuff for Britney, but he couldn't imagine himself going there with all his guards. He decided to tell them that they could go home.

As he approached them, they all started getting into the vehicles in preparation for the homeward journey. He paused them in their tracks. "Please, I won't be needing the services of all of you for the evening. There is something I have to do this evening, and I don't think that it's a good idea showing up there with all of you. All of you can go home except Carlos, who is to drive me."

His bodyguards were puzzled. They wondered where he was going that made him not require their services. He was the one who had asked for them to be sent to him, to accompany him everywhere he went because he was scared of another attack and all of a sudden, he asked them to withdraw for the evening. They got into the Mercedes S600 Guard and zoomed off. They knew that asking questions was not allowed.

"So, where is this classified location, boss?"

Deshawn laughed loudly, holding his ribs. "You never cease to amaze me Carlos. I never said it was a classified location. I only said I didn't want many people with me."

Carlos started the ignition, "Where to?"

"To the mall."

Carlos pulled into the mall and parked the car. Deshawn got down and started heading towards the entrance. Deshawn looked over his shoulder and saw Carlos following him.

"Why are you following me Carlos?" Deshawn asked.

"Nothing, boss. You know that your usual bodyguards are not here. I felt it was necessary to follow you, just in case," Carlos said. He shrugged his shoulders and added, "You never can tell."

"So, who's going to watch the car?"

"Forget about the car. You're more important."

"So, what if someone plants a bomb underneath the car while we're away?" Deshawn asked, the corner of his lips curling up in a smile.

Carlos knew he was joking around and laughed in response to the question.

Inside the mall, Deshawn headed for the toy store. His face flushed with embarrassment as he stuffed several baskets with everything he thought a little girl would like. He felt somewhat relieved that Carlos did not ask any questions, that would have added to the awkwardness of the situation. He had always been very confident and prided himself in always knowing what to say and do, to be the leader in every situation. He hated awkward situations where he felt exposed and not so confident.

After shopping, he and Carlos stuffed the car with the six hundred dollars' worth of presents and clothes. Deshawn had to squeeze himself in the front seat, with a giant purple unicorn on his lap.

"Where to boss?" Carlos asked.

Carlos sounded relaxed and comfortable, like they always went out to shop for toys and presents. Carlos's question reminded Deshawn of something else that he didn't really think about. How the hell was he going to get the presents to his daughter? Carlos didn't know about her or B'onca.

He glanced at his watch, it was almost seven at night.

"Go to the 4th Street Charlotte Park," he instructed Carlos.

As Carlos navigated the car to the location he had said, Deshawn took out the phone he used to communicate with B'onca and turned it on. There were tons of missed calls and text notifications that popped up. He ignored the notifications, and dialed her number. It rang for a while before she picked.

"Hey, can you meet me across the street at the park in 20 minutes?"

B'onca's voice was so loud, that Deshawn was sure Carlos could hear it from where he sat in front.

"What the hell Shawn? I'm about to leave for work."

"This late at night? Who's watching Britney?"

"Since when do you care?" B'onca fired back, there was an icy edge to her tone.

"Well, I am her father and I do care."

He heard B'onca scoff on the other end.

"B'onca please, just tell me."

"Well, if you must know, I've been picking up extra night shifts at the hospital a couple of nights a week. My mother is in town for Britney's birthday party tomorrow, so she'd be watching her tonight, but I pay Miss Margaret to come and stay the night with her on other nights."

"Who is Margaret? And why are you picking up extra shifts, didn't I leave you guys enough money the last time I visited?"

"I do not have time to have this conversation with you right now. I don't want to be late for work."

Deshawn wanted answers to his questions, but he remembered that wasn't his reason for calling her in the first place. He decided to let the matter rest.

"Well, I have a couple of gifts to give you for Britney's party tomorrow. Can you just bring your car across the street in a few minutes? We're almost there."

For some seconds neither of them spoke.

"Fine, I'll meet you there," then she hung up.

When Deshawn and Carlos pulled up at the park, B'onca was already there waiting for them. Carlos helped Deshawn make several trips from their car to hers with all the gifts. Deshawn thought that B'onca would be happy seeing all the stuff that he got for their daughter. But she just stood with her hand on her hip, shaking her head every time he brought another bag. When they were done with the transfer, Carlos returned to the driver's seat of their vehicle and left Deshawn and B'onca alone.

"You don't look happy," Deshawn observed.

"Should I be happy?" B'onca asked haughtily.

"Can't you see all the nice presents that I bought our daughter?"

"And so fucking what Deshawn? You think you can abscond from your fatherly duties and then try to cover it up with money?"

"It's not like that B'onca."

"Then how is it Shawn?" She asked. "You tell me. You rarely ever spend time with your daughter. You come in when she is asleep and then dump money on the kitchen counter. Is the money supposed to take your place in her life? Is the money supposed to become her father?"

By the time she finished she was almost shouting at the top of her voice.

Deshawn understood how she felt. "B'onca I really love our daughter, I do. I always try my best to provide for her to the best of my ability. Can't you see all the nice stuff I bought her for her party?" Deshawn said, gesturing to B'onca's car which had been stuffed full with presents. "I love Britney very much," he continued, "I'd love to spend time with her, but the nature of my job does not permit me to."

B'onca looked at him like she would spit.

"What kind of job keeps a father away from his child. Whatever job it is that you do that keeps you away from your daughter, resign from it," B'onca said.

"B'onca you know I can't do that."

"What job is it that you do anyway?"

"It's complicated."

B'onca moved closer to him. Her voice had become lower and she no longer shouted at him. She took hold of his arm.

"Shawn, why are you keeping secrets from me? Why don't you want to let me in? You can trust me."

"B'onca this thing is deeper than you think."

"Tell me, I will understand," she kept pressing.

Tears were starting to gather in her eyes. It was obvious that soon she was going to have an emotional breakdown and Deshawn didn't want to be there when it happened. He might be moved out of pity for her, to confide in her. That was something he was not ready to do, at least not yet.

"I have to go now," he said.

Without saying goodbye or waiting for her to say goodbye, he turned and headed back to the car.

The tears flowed down B'onca's cheeks. She was both frustrated and confused. She shouted his name several times as he walked away, but he didn't answer her or even turn around.

When Deshawn got into his car, he sat and waited till he saw B'onca get in her own car and drive off.

Carlos looked at Deshawn through the rearview mirror. Deshawn looked tired like someone who carried a weight he could not shake off from his shoulders. His face looked sad, Carlos could not tell what was saddening him, but he knew it was a private matter. He didn't ask any questions. If Deshawn wanted to discuss it with him, he would do so of his own accord.

Without turning around, Carlos asked, "Where to now?"

"Take me home."

Deshawn relaxed into the soft leather of the vehicle, resting his head on the head rest. He looked out the car window, staring at the lit-up streets as the car sped homeward.

On the morning of his daughter's birthday, Deshawn thought about giving her another birthday present. One that she might never know of, but one that would give him peace of mind. It was something he had been planning for a while, but on impulse, he decided to do it that morning. He only hoped that everything would work out perfectly like it had done in his head.

He picked up his phone and called Sammy when he got to the office. He told Sammy to meet him within the hour.

Twenty minutes later Sammy arrived in a black shirt with polka dots and denim jeans. His jaw looked clean shaven like someone who just shaved that morning. He shook hands with Deshawn and took a seat.

"Do you know why I called you here Sammy?" Deshawn began.

"No," Sammy replied.

"I've been gathering intel, and I think it's time to act," Deshawn said. He relaxed more into his seat and continued, "I have eyes on Don Li. From the intel that I've gathered, he follows a pretty routine schedule. He leaves his house by half past seven and arrives to his office by eight. The drive takes him more than thirty minutes on some days. He stays in his office, and does not leave until it's four o'clock. He leaves his office before four only when there is something urgent he has to attend to in person. When he gets home, he changes and leaves to play badminton at the sports club. Sometimes, he plays table tennis in his house. On days that he visits the sports club, he usually returns home by seven or past seven in the evening." Deshawn paused his speech and looked at Sammy's face.

"Go on," Sammy said.

"Now the thing is, I have always known that one day Don Li was going to become a threat to our business, but I did not imagine it would be this soon. I have been gathering information about him for quite a long time now. I have always been waiting for the right time to use it, but it seems that no time could be more right than now."

Deshawn paused his speech and drank from the glass in front of him. "We have always been on the defensive side in our encounters with him," he continued. "Though somehow we have always managed to get the better of him," Deshawn rubbed his hands together as he spoke. "I want that to change. I do not want us to keep being on the defensive. I want us to strike him now. He lost many men and he wouldn't be expecting us to bring the fight to him. That is why we must attack first and put an end to his interference in our business."

"What must I do?" Sammy asked.

"Good," Deshawn said. "Tom is the one who has been digging up the information for me. He is already heading to the location, you are to wait for Don Li to emerge from the sports club. Tom will text you the location. He usually leaves the sports club by seven, so be there by half past six. Tom and Jamie will mount surveillance on the building till you join them there with more men. I want you to take Don Li out. He is becoming a pain in the ass, and I think it's time someone takes out the trash. Do you understand me?"

"More than you think," Sammy said. "I'll attend to some things that need urgent attention, then I'll join Tom and Jamie as soon as possible."

"That's good."

Sammy stood up to leave the room, before Deshawn's voice halted him in his tracks.

"Sammy," Deshawn called and Sammy turned around. "Bring me good news."

Sammy nodded and then left the room.

Deshawn sank deeper into his chair and closed his eyes. Don Li wouldn't be expecting him to attack, at least not so soon. He wanted to give him a surprise. One that he would remember in the afterlife. He had decided to carry out the attack on Don Li on his daughter's birthday because, for all he knew, Don Li was one of the biggest threats to his daughter and B'onca. It would be nice if his daughter could grow up in a Don Li free world. That was why he made up his mind, rather impulsively, to hit Don Li that day. He busied himself with work, until Sammy reported back to him.

Tom and Jamie sat patiently in the car, waiting for Don Li to come out of the sports club. Tom was the one behind the wheel. They had been waiting for over an hour. From where they were parked, they could see Don Li's cars with some of his men waiting next to them. The plan was to launch a direct attack on both Don Li and his bodyguards and take Don Li out for good. But, they had to wait for Sammy and the rest of the boys to join them.

They were still waiting when they saw Don Li step out of the sports club. Jamie glanced at his wristwatch, it was only quarter to six. They wondered why Don Li was suddenly leaving early – had someone tipped him off? He was descending the steps of the sports club, heading towards his car.

"Fuck!" Tom shouted, and banged the steering.

"Why is he leaving early?" Jamie asked no one in particular, and raised his hand in frustration.

"Get your gun Jamie," Tom instructed.

"What?"

"Get your fucking gun. I'm going to drive over there and you're going to shoot the fucking bastard."

"Aren't we supposed to wait for the others?" Jamie asked, confused.

"Fuck the others. I can't let him get away."

Tommy started the car. By now, Don Li was almost to the bottom of the steps. Jamie pulled out an AK 47 rifle that had been lying on the floor of the car, next to his feet. As Tom raced towards their target, he checked the gun in readiness to fire.

Don Li had been in the sports club playing badminton. He had gotten thirsty, and gone to have a drink when he saw his phone's notification light flashing. On impulse, he picked up the phone and saw a text. *Leave there now.* He quickly packed up and told his boys that were with him that it was time to leave.

He hurried out of the sports club and down the stairs. He had gotten to the last stair and was making his way towards the car when a red car drove by and slowed down. He saw a man lift a rifle and aim it at him. The next thing he heard was the sound of rapid gunfire that filled the air. He dove for cover, but one of his guards standing next to him was hit in the chest. The car zoomed off immediately.

Don Li felt something dripping on the floor beside him. It was his blood. He had been hit twice in the side by the bullets. The adrenaline rush of the moment had made him numb to the hit. Two of his men came to him and helped him into the car while the other men pursued the red car.

Tom and Jamie had already gone a considerable distance and taken a couple of turns before Don Li's men could recover from the shock of the attack and pursue them. Jamie lowered the rifle to his side.

"Do you think you got him?" Tom asked.

"Yeah, I'm positive about that. I just don't know exactly where I got him."

Tom peered into the rearview mirror to make sure that no car was following them, something had told him that Don Li's men would attempt to come after them. But he didn't see anyone. Don Li's men had started pursuing too late and couldn't figure out which direction they took.

Jamie took out his phone and dialed Sammy's number.

"Sammy, the deal is off. We are en-route to safe house one. Meet us there."

Then he ended the call and stared in front of him as Tom drove.

Deshawn was still in the office ten minutes to seven. He wanted to leave, but couldn't until Sammy came back to give him a report. Deshawn didn't know whether to expect good news or bad news. So, he sat in his office, watching television and twirling the remote control around in his hand though his mind was far away from the images displayed on the screen. When the tension became too much, he got up and poured himself a glass of wine. Wine always calmed him down, it would give him the patience to wait.

Deshawn looked at the door when the handle turned, and Sammy came into the room. Deshawn waved him to a seat hurriedly, eager to know how everything went.

"So, how did it go Sammy?" Deshawn asked, barely waiting for him to sit down.

"I was on my way to the sports club with about five men when Jamie called and said that the deal was off, that I should meet them at safe house one. When I got there, I was told that Don Li came out of the club before it was six o'clock."

"The damned mole at it again," Deshawn whispered fiercely.

"I hadn't gotten to the sports club yet, so Jamie and Tom did a drive by shooting in an attempt to take out Don Li."

"And?"

"And I'm convinced that they hit him. Jamie says he's positive that he got him more than once."

Deshawn's face lit up with a broad smile. This was the news he had been waiting for all day. He stood up and got another glass for Sammy, and then poured him some wine. He couldn't hide his excitement at the news.

"I must say that I am impressed with the way that Tom and Jamie handled the situation," Deshawn said.

Sammy took the glass which Deshawn had filled halfway.

"Let's toast to the demise of Don Li," Deshawn said, lifting his glass.

"And to better business days," Sammy added before they clinked glasses.

They sat in Deshawn's office watching television and drinking wine until it was about eight at night. When they realized how long they had been at the office, they got up and Sammy waited by the door while Deshawn tidied up. They went downstairs together, Sammy walked towards his car and Deshawn got into his own car.

As Deshawn settled into the back seat of his vehicle, his phone vibrated. He unlocked the phone and opened the message. He froze as he saw the content of the message. His heart started pounding and his hands became sweaty, he had to tighten his grip on the phone to prevent it from slipping through his hand. He could feel blood or water, or whatever it was, rush into his ears and fill his head. Suddenly the whole car began to go around in circles and he dropped his phone on the seat. The phone's screen was still glowing, with the message displayed on it.

We know about B'onca.